Do Princesses and Super Heroes Hit the Trails?

A NATIONAL PARK ADVENTURE

Carmela LaVigna Coyle Illustrated by Mike Gordon

MUDDY BOOTS

Guilford, Connecticut

Published by Muddy Boots
An imprint of Globe Pequot

Distributed by NATIONAL BOOK NETWORK

British Library Cataloguing-in-Publication Information available

Library of Congress Control Number: 2016911787

ISBN 978-1-63076-244-5 (hardcover)

ISBN 978-1-63076-245-2 (e-book)

♾™ The paper used in this publication meets the minimum requirements of American
National Standard for Information Sciences—Permanence of Paper for Printed Library
Materials, ANSI/NISO Z39.48-1992.

Do Princesses and Super Heroes Hit the Trails?

A NATIONAL PARK ADVENTURE

Carmela LaVigna Coyle *Illustrated by Mike Gordon*

MUDDY BOOTS

Guilford, Connecticut

Published by Muddy Boots
An imprint of Globe Pequot

Distributed by NATIONAL BOOK NETWORK

British Library Cataloguing-in-Publication Information available

Library of Congress Control Number: 2016911787

ISBN 978-1-63076-244-5 (hardcover)

ISBN 978-1-63076-245-2 (e-book)

∞™ The paper used in this publication meets the minimum requirements of American
National Standard for Information Sciences—Permanence of Paper for Printed Library
Materials, ANSI/NISO Z39.48-1992.

For Andrea (the new girl in my life)
and her enthusiasm for hitting the trails.
—clvc

To my two princesses, Hannah and Melissa,
who always remind me of how fun life can be.
—MG

What can we do for a *super* fun day?

The national parks look like a good place to play.

Do super heroes ride mules down into the canyon?

If this princess can be your riding companion.

I hope we see salamanders, toads,
and some frogs!

I hear they like living near moss-covered logs.

Does this road really go all the way to the sun?

How do we know when
Old Faithful will blow?

We just have to wait for an hour . . . or so.

The Great Smoky Mountains have flowers galore!

Let's take THIS trail and begin to explore.

GREAT SMOKY MOUNTAINS
★ NATIONAL PARK ★

I LOVE the sea creatures
on Acadia's shore!

We **HAVE** to come back and investigate more.

Never-ever have I EVER seen a moose.

I think there's one hiding
behind that blue spruce!

ROCKY MOUNTAIN
★ NATIONAL PARK ★

Where do we go for the BEST canyon views?

We'll wade up the Narrows in our new water shoes.

★ ZION ★
NATIONAL PARK

Take a picture of this cactus and me!

Say "SUPER HERO" on the count of three.

It moved through this tube to the ocean below.

HAWAI'I VOLCANOES
★ NATIONAL PARK ★

That snowy mountain is poking the sky.

Denali is almost four miles high!

★ DENALI ★
NATIONAL PARK

Sometimes I can't find the words in my head.

Maybe it's okay to be silent instead.

There are national parks
all over the nation!

DID YOU KNOW?

GRAND CANYON

"Kaibab," the Paiute Indian word for the Grand Canyon, means "mountain turned upside down."

OLYMPIC

There are three diverse ecosystems in Olympic National Park: coastal, temperate rainforest, and mountain-meadow. That's why some people say it's like visiting three parks in one.

GLACIER

In 1850 there were an estimated 150 glaciers in Glacier National Park. Today there are only 25 remaining in the park vicinity.

YELLOWSTONE

Yellowstone, established in 1872 by President Grant, was the very first national park.

GREAT SMOKY

This park never sleeps! It's open 24 hours a day, 365 days a year. It's also the most visited of all the national parks.

ACADIA

Thunder Hole, a large rock formation along the coast, makes the clapping sound of thunder when waves crash over it.

ROCKY MOUNTAIN

Trail Ridge Road at 12,183 feet above sea level is the highest through-road in the nation.

ZION

In 2002, the Olympic Torch was carried through Zion on its way to Salt Lake City's opening ceremony and games.

SAGUARO

Ancient petroglyphs (also known as rock carvings) were pecked into the rocks by Hohokam people over 1000 years ago.

HAWAI'I VOLCANOES

Sometimes it snows on top of the volcanic mountain of Mauna Loa!

DENALI

Caribou, very similar to reindeer, live in and wander Denali most of the year.

YOSEMITE

Yosemite has countless waterfalls, endless valleys, and some of the tallest and oldest trees on earth!

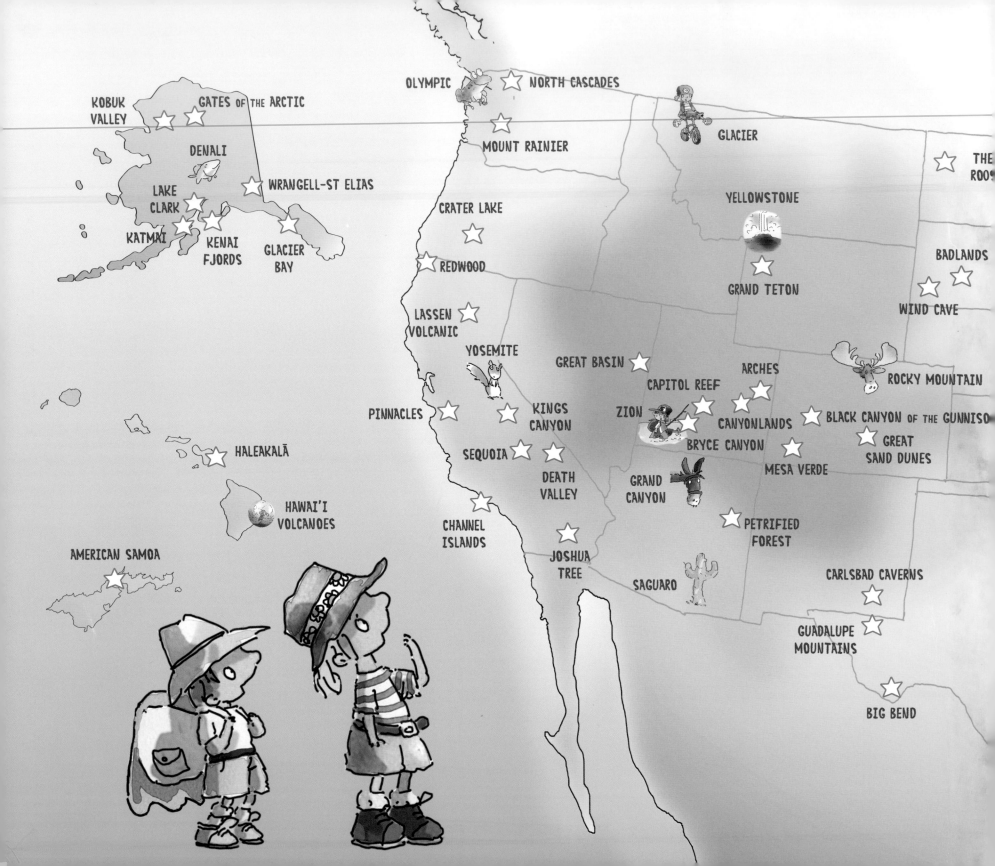